Sexsensual

To: Corinne

Pharaoh Robinson

Thank you for the Love & Support

2/17/2011

www.*Sexsensual*.biz
Pharaoh.Robinson@gmail.com

This book is a work of fiction. The poetry, names, characters, and plots are all fictitious creations of the author's imagination.

ISBN 10: 0615392482
ISBN 13: 9780615392486

First Printing: 2010

Book cover Design: Darnell Loper
Book cover Photography: Pharaoh Robinson

This book was printed in the United States of America

Sexsensual

The King of Erotica

Pharaoh Robinson

Sexsensual Contents

Acknowledgements

First and foremost, I thank God for my poetic gift. I am who I am through Him. To all the beautiful women, especially my beautiful black women, I love the very essence of you. I hope you find serenity and comfort in my words. I hope you mentally make love to my poetic music, called *Sexsensual*. Don't hold back your mental inhibitions in reading my work, let yourself go. If you end up introducing your hidden alter ego or mental fetish to your husband or man, may he scream in ecstasy and be forever lost under your spell, in your book of pleasure principles.

For all the black women that have molded me into the man that I am and striving to become, I thank you. This book is dedicated to the hopeless romantics, the sensual, the sexual and the romantically inhibited. May you read this book and let your mind go within these pages to places of fantasy. From these words, may you create your own flights of fantasy.

This book is also dedicated to my 5th grade teacher Mrs. Jones. I thank you for introducing me to the art form known as poetry. You planted a seed that life and time has cultivated. This book is only a fraction of my life with more great things to come.

I would like to give a special thank you to my editors Aisha Duncan, Marsha Epps and Charleá Jackson. I appreciate your support, patience and professionalism. This book is going to print, because of you. I couldn't have done it without you.

To all of my *Tagged.com* friends and fans, you have truly inspired, loved, supported and encouraged me. This is our book, our journey and I thank you for motivating me to follow my dream and not allow me to lay it down.

For my daughters, my babies, my princesses, my queens to be: Daddy will be your example of what a true man should be. I will be your first date, your first idea of chivalry and your first gentleman.

To my little sisters, Nikki and Aja, I love you. You've been such great inspirations to me. I, in turn, hope that I have been a great big brother and beautiful black man. Thank you for all the love, support and advice.

And lastly, to my mother, the woman who through example, prayer, spankings and love, has molded me into the man that I am, I thank you. I love you. I know you will not be reading this book, however I look forward to you reading some of my more conscious poetry. That book is coming soon!

A *Sexsensual* Man

It is said, that the ability of a man to love a woman, is nowhere to be found today. Today's representation of "Black Love" is more than the exploitation of how we treat our women. Black is beautiful, and this book of prose is my contribution to our "Beautiful." From our smiles, to our smooth walks, to the eclectic way we chose to talk and navigate in this world. This is my "Black Cool" tool.

This is my genesis of New Love. Enjoy a new renaissance of romance, sensuality, sexuality, chivalry, fantasy and erotica from a masculine voice catering to the femininity in the playground of a woman's mind. Here a man can love a woman's mind and a woman can allow herself to mentally be loved and explore her unknown horizons.

Men, if you are at a loss for words to express your sexuality, sensuality, romance, love and erotic voice, use mine. The power of mental stimulation communication and attention are the keys to finding your fantasy woman, within your woman.

May these words be the verbal Sexsensual mental therapy that opens doors and releases the flood gates of passion for you and her to explore. For that, I give you Sexsensual.

Sexsensual

"All things Sexsensual may not be meant to be acted out, nor should they be repressed in the confines of the mind and never sorted out."

- Pharaoh Robinson

Preface

Women love men who love women. This is a quintessential truth that binds strong relationships together. It is also the premise that has given birth to the poems in this book. Sexsensual is a tangible out of body experience. An intimate ellipse, of what one man has to offer women with erotic palates. Pharaoh Robinson is an outspoken poet and writer. He has created a series of fantasies and experiences, for those whom embrace their sexuality.

In this realm, his pen is definitely mightier than the sword. No inhibitions will be left behind. These poems will expose themselves to you, without apology. Each poem will command your attention and you may even find yourself aroused, while turning the pages. By no means is this collection of poetry, a simplistic showcase of stanzas about relationships. It is more than a one sided conversation about sex. It is however, an unveiling of what we say and do in the dark.

For years, people have shared their lives of eroticism through words, through poetry. Not until now, has there been such a poet to demonstrate the rawness and power behind those words. Pharaoh Robinson is committed to being both the giver and the receiver. He has taken the essence of who we are, as lovers, and created an outlet for us to be our true selves. I can assure you that, Sexsensual will satisfy the deepest of your desires.

Aisha Duncan
Poet / Author

http://www.southafrica.info/about/history/saartjie.htm

Saartjie "Sarah" Baartman was Khoi Khoi woman who was taken from South Africa, and then exhibited as a freak across Britain. The image and idea of "The Hottentot Venus" swept through British popular culture. A court battle waged by abolitionists to free her from her exhibitors failed.

Baartman was sold to a Frenchman, who took her to France. An animal trainer, Regu, exhibited her under more pressured conditions for fifteen months. French naturalists, among them Georges Cuvier, visited her and she was the subject of several scientific paintings at the Jardin du Roi, where she was examined in March 1815: as Saint-Hilaire and Frédéric Cuvier, a younger brother of Georges, reported, "She was obliging enough to undress and to allow herself to be painted in the nude." Once her novelty had worn off on Parisians, she began to drink heavily and support herself with prostitution.

She died the next year. But even after her death, Sara Baartman remained an object of imperialist scientific investigation. In the name of Science, her sexual organs and brain were displayed in the Musee de l'Homme in Paris until as recently as 1985.

http://icarusfilms.com/new99/hottento.html)

"For so long my women have been kept in the dark, made to be seen as ugly, inelegant, scientifically odd and distasteful in appearance. May the world see, feel, taste, touch, and experience Black Beauty. In all its voluptuous, full, succulent, erotic, sensual, sexual splendor called Black Woman. I make love to you my Sara Baartmans."

- Pharaoh Robinson

I Make Love to: Saartjie "Sarah" Baartman

She is chocolate milk
My thick heavenly silk
Don't reduce an ounce of her fat
Give me my Africa in jet black
I love her Cape Coast alpha curves
Take my tongue across her sweetest nerves
I kiss those places, where they made fun of her

Black labia clamshell black pearl
Plump dark nipple relaxed and ripe
I take in my mouth and suckle Eros
No media attention or followers needed
Never oversexed
She and I make love without sex
Rhythmically rolling her hips
Sweet watermelon full lips as she walks

When I can't have her
I dream her up in variations
Softly eating caramel pussy on stick
Riding red bones highs deep into my nights
I rub down southern brown earth-tone thighs
Tonight I am naked with a big beautiful mulatto
Last night black coal kaleidoscope legs wrap me 'til I begged

Sometimes we are Congo drums
That dance with rhythmical feet
In mystical dirt sweaty and beautiful until I hurts
Beating bodies coming until we hum
I make love to it, I make love to her I make love to them
Round full lips, rotund black hips

Until they sashay and sway soulfully away

We make sextory, birthing exotic little stories
In multiple shades of beautiful black
You are the naked history lost
Due to sticky pages over the ages
Swallowing the heart of many men
Silently men fantasized from multiple nations
With exotic curiosity that sped the hearts velocity
Going on mental sexual vacation to your places
To make love to the daughters
That I love, and hold up above

I say again with mental images of over-curved
Black beauties with sexual nerve that unearth
Walking around with the world on their backs I make love to it,
I make love to her
I make love to them
I make love to the daughters of Saartjie Baartman

Sexsensual

Embodied
This hook of life
Sing this lifetime with me
Melodically in love methodically

Our bodies move in conversation, no need to talk
Ingredients like these blend heavenly
This sweet spontaneity is blind
Uninformed minds that never telegraph
Geniuses of the left and right side of Love's mind

Infinite nights with you are needed, past lifetime
To absorb the soul we need to put into this
Our internal clocks, shoplift time
From Father Time, secretly on this love we press rewind

Once, we almost receded away
Erotic cerebral beings washed away
Animalistic soulfully tamed meanings
Sexually we must momentarily dominate
Sensually we must find a way to constantly recreate
The *Sexsensual* elements that are forever relevant

Black Body Blues

Sweet Southern Belle
Make me yell,
Give me a back alley yell

Stroke the blues in my soul
Kiss me with the rhythm in your hips

Give me that Mo' Betta
Hot melting butter love
Like no otha'

Wrap your legs around my neck
Savory chocolate, vanilla thighs
Black Tom Cruise lost in heaven
Drownin' in black skies

Put roots on me
Chalk me with your walk
Shake that chicken-leg love
Red sauce love, thick like bayou love

Stroke the blues in my soul
Kiss me with the rhythm in your hips

Black lovin'
Sweetly drug me silly
Southern heroin in yo' hips
Soul sista voo-doo black sweating delight

Sweet Southern Belle
Make me yell,
Give me a back-alley yell

Mind Sex

Come with me
Close your eyes
Get naked with me
Press it against me roughly

Remove nothing
Yet strip everything
Bare yourself nudely
Lick me, then bite me rudely

Remove your inhibitions
Unloosen it, until unconformity
Wrap your legs around me in unity
Get used to me

Allow me to fondle your soul
Caress the nipples of your mental breast
Breathe my breath, cinnamon sweet
My lips slowly swimming upstream

French kiss me mentally
Stimulate me hard
Deep throat me verbally
Never touch me, but give me touch

We will climax through eye contact
Black bodies in hot sweats created mentally
Muted orgasms scratch my back, in my mind
Wrap your legs around my mind, squeeze me tight

Kiss me, but don't kiss me
Touch me, but don't touch me
Caress me, but don't caress me

Warm gushes from mental pushes
Squirting hot joy you coat my mind
Slushy wet in my mind, you grip and ride
Climax until euphoric intoxicated sex highs.

Fuck me, like I'm there, without touch
Suck me, wet your throat mentally quench yourself
Taste your nectar off your finger tips thick like it is me
Scream as you beam up mentally in extraterrestrial dreams

Let me fuck you, but not fuck you
Let me choke you, but not choke you
Let me stroke you deeply, but not stroke you
But don't let me touch you . . .

Sugar Water

Bring it on like spring rain
Let me feel your seasons change
Dancing lips in your downpours
Addicted to the cane in your sugar roots
Sweet tooth drug addict runs soul deep

Your sugar water well is a necessity
Rubber band veins scream my name
Tie me off tight a dream ride tonight
Undeniable to the fraction of this chemistry
I can't kick this or you, a willing victim with no remedy

Recede your tide, relinquish your hold
I need to run blindly away and go forever cold
This is the last wave I ride, no more tonight
Give me back my thought, my sweet serenity
Dry mouthed thirst for seconds of your soaked pleasure

I eat to reminisce
It is a necessity to taste you
Yes I dance with my face wet
Under umbrella thighs spread wide
In the rain taking naked mouth body baths

Like yesterday's sweet pussy blues
I fiend for you like tomorrow's good news
Moving me like black magic dancing shoes
Oh how I love that sugar water thing you got in you

Eclectic Candy Electric

Let's be
Eclectic candy electric
Waves of new creativity that role-play abstract realities

Sending assorted sexual electricity
From our cerebral erotic cities through our bodies
Sensual drips on our tongue's tips, as sweet soul sweat glitters
We don't silence or flee, nor will we sexually convulse, from our erotic jitters

Let's be
Eclectic candy electric
Mental sweet spots in our sexual sensual mental wonderland

Let's unwrap this mental third-eye new world candy-land
Softly palate each other, sweet, salty, sour, engulfing as we unnerve
Bittersweet tangy salutes, lapping away today to savor tomorrow's taste
Release that animalistic beast, unwrap that sweetly foiled thing labeled
"Sexsensual"

Let's be
Eclectic candy electric
Four-play with no hands, just tongues that run, bondage for fun
This is an erotic computation
Imaginative mutation
New creation of an erotic nation

Purple Pussy Blues

She is electric guitar string legs
Wrapped around juke joint smoke
Dancing on Love Street in black sweat
Purple pussy rhythms on a mahogany stick
She is corn whiskey strong Chicago cold syrup thick

"I sing her purple pussy blues and drink her rhythm 'til I'm drunk"

She's my drunken drum-set, beaded doorway blues
Beating black molasses asses, thick as cold syrup
She is the epitome, my midnight song
Black snake moan bring it home
She is the sensuous suck
Amorphously contorting me
She is everything I can't hold

"I sing her purple pussy blues and drink her rhythm 'til I'm drunk"

She is southern vertical lips
My Miss Mississippi moonshine
Tantalizing ass
Eyes open wide
When I lick it from behind
She is sweet liquefied
Ceaseless
Sanctified satisfaction
When she throws' it back
I might change my last name
To her last name
Just call me
Mr. Jackson

"I sing her purple pussy blues and drink her rhythm 'til I'm drunk"

Illegal Access

If you grant me access into your recess
Understand this will haunt you like rote memory
Repetitive relics painting a thousand faces of me
Let me stream my campaign, giving you sweet pain
I will make your late night memoirs, my new residential
Uninhibited personalities will no longer be kept confidential

Believe the unbelievable whole-heartedly perceive the unperceivable
This can't be understood in English, close your mouth, and speak no replies
Understand psychologically I am the anti-virus in violation like mental sexual piracy
Blind to the human eye use your mind, this is illegal access close your eyes to witness this
My personalities are alter egos, like altered minds, changing your perception love's conception

Black Stick Voodoo

Watch me work this root
Black licorice vine of mine
Physiological mind strokes so divine
Sweetest mojo' you know, no joke, just lick the spoon
Stirring your chocolate soup, injections of sweetmeat confections

I am your Black Voodoo Stick
Midnight chicken leg, shakin' bayou's bed
So thick, so ridiculous, inhale this mental rush

So Omega
The end of the beginning
Let me take ya', deep into this
Erotic of pot gumbo of mental sexual ingredient bliss
Open up and take thick black candy, brown sugar cane straight

I am black banana thick, jambalaya lips
Voodoo king take this sweet-water cornbread kiss
All in the name of love's greatest drug, black voodoo sex
Black sweat no rest; make your alley cat scream, scratches on my back
Pin sticking love, g-spot balloon burst, everglade squirt, scream 'til it hurts

And remember this . . . Black Voodoo Stick
Midnight chicken leg, shakin' bayou's bed
So thick, so ridiculous, inhale this mental rush

Climax Pill

Take me at your own risk
And let me be your narcoleptic narcotic
Of screaming impaired double vision climax
Your sweet deviation of cataplexy sexual seizures
Slurping you into slurred speech of subdued context

Clutch your legs with pre-cream conditions
Then play me back to experience me in renditions
Ignore your conscience pleading you to leave this bad habit be
I am the hot delirium that makes your pussy convulse and hallucinate
You are not crazy when you hear talking voices from between your legs

Midnight whispers that break you off in your sleep
Hot flashes as your body thrashes, fucking my shadow to sleep
The idiomatic actor inside you indoctrinate it's self repeatedly with me
Oppressed silhouettes in dream state, exploit your nights as you find sexual freedom
Wet windowpane invisible images of me, your sweet rain man you Kegel me like your hand

You see, I am your Sexsensual psycho Eros therapist
Disabling your paranoia feeding multiple-orgasmic cornucopia
Chills run deep with orgasm-amphetamine that squirts
compulsively Substance abuse screams with tactile twitches of Schizophrenic pussy lips
I am your body's perfectionist you are habitually addicted to me

Don't Fight It

Let me release you
Drown you, in you
Unleash yourself on you
Manifest erotic thoughts deeply
Found in your crevice, erotically resurface
With your own lips, kiss yourself off my lips

Let me untie your mind
Unravel your erotic personality
Release your narcissistic selfish sex
In streams of thick cream on me, take it deeply
The mental touch and mind suck

Don't fight it
Climax deep internal on it
Give into it as you swim in it
Orgasmic lagoons, of erotic self bliss
Use me to release it, embrace it until you
Cease to exist here, let me take you there in it
Spread the legs of your mind and take flight, don't fight it

I Can Touch You

500 thread count sheets
Lay your body down on me
Silk, satin, velvet become me

Strong fervent flavor
Taste your morning coffee
Black like me
Savor your sensual breakfast

Extended cream when you scream
Golden faucets in falsetto
Streaming trickles of my love water
Romance past reality bathes your spiritually

Rose petals flying
Vanilla swirls the air
Bathing your body slowly
Extensively day by day
Close your eyes and touch me

On my knees, massaging your body
Mentally, I never leave
Spiritually surpass physicality
Sensually at night you become me

Hallucinating restlessly
You still wrestle with me
Soulfully I can still touch you

Let Me Have You

You inhale me in your sleep
Resounding echo of my voice
An exhaling smile of peaceful rejoice
Deeply you hug nothing and feel me

Naked bodies and bare feet
Dancing until our bodies are moist
Make love to me as if you had no choice
Dream of a scream and passion until you weep

Let me have you my love
Mind, body, dream and all
Paint on the walls of your mind
My captive stolen angel from above
Let me have my love, hear my beckoning call
Kiss Father Time, until he gives you the keys of time

Insatiable

Spreading ecstasy's legs, sweetly stretching her limits
Reminiscent soul caress, artistic tongues painting
Erotic languages, speak on lingering lips
With angled acoustic licks
Orgasm screamed
Dancing in nectar's stream
Vibrate internal, external Cream

Licking signatures, on abstract walls
Dipping in your black body ink
I compose curling toes that squeeze
Romance out of the wind

Talk to me
In speech impediment baritone tongues
Addictively chasing my lips
Sweetwater brown sugar cane
Southern thighs calling my name

Acoustics singing naked body blues
Crying tears of abandoned love
REM sleep wet dreams of me

You are a self-touching mime
Your bed it is erotic abandonment
You act as a sensual impressionist of me
A sexual ventriloquist playing me
Irrational wet sheets stubbornly cling to you
Devoid of me

You are
Insatiably
Unsatisfied without me. . .

iSex

Upload this psychological mind suck

Star track orgasms that leave your body on earth
Fellatio multiple ratio mind screaming squirt dreams
Catatonic electric twitch, meaningless phrases you repeat

I am your hetero oral sexual program
Be my face-sitting flexible functional keyboard
Give me iHead over the edge
Deep throat version point of no return
I love your trademark no hands no choke
Electronic energy lips that slurp

We use our face to interface
I love the relativity of this sexual connectivity
While you handstand, I lick your console
Sixty-nine bit graphic tongue work
As you re-load catch your breath
Then Ctrl-Alt—Delete me to completion

Hands-free riding, eye contact talk to me
iLuv you like hyperactivity sweet tooth cavities
Work this thick joystick, Bluetooth body compatibility
Download all over me, screaming until your systems crash

We are exhausted in iLuv
Slick lathered gamers
Sex machines with battery sweat
Drained with low charge
Until we recharge, re-start iMoan
You scream and we iSex

Make It Talk to Me

Erotic impulsive
Uninhibited thought
Knees bent
Arms out-stretched
Back arched deep on all fours

Bound and restricted wrist
Blind-folded spread out on the floor
Spontaneous with a twist
Blind hesitation
Sensual contemplation

Deep voice, a soft whisper . . . "Do as I say, enjoy what I do."

The trickle of honey warm sticky and thick
Gliding from the crease of your pretty brown round
A warm tongue gliding in reverse
Up your spine tracing a sensual curse
As fingers play the clit like piano keys
Erotic sensations. . . silence a pause time

Deep voice, a soft whisper. . . "Arch It Up . . ."

Warm tongue taking you from behind
Lapping at your black pearl and creamy folds
Restrained hands reaching for sheets that don't exist
Losing control in search of more
Yet blind to everything

Deep voice, a soft whisper. . . "You want more?"

On the peak of climax yearning for penetration
I slide in slow, press deep and pause to enjoy the moan
Clinched fist, and gritted teeth you take it
As I increase the pace . . . soft, yet thunderous
Painful yet blissful

Room moving in slow motion she contracts
Squeezing and pulsating
Powerfully she Kegels me
Softly she creams for me
Language unknown she talks to me
You lose and scream for me
She clinches and releases me

Deep voice, a soft whisper . . . "I like to make your kitten talk to me."

Increased speeds . . . buckling knees
Your fingers work like sign language for
something to hold Body in vibration . . . she's
losing control
Stutters, spasms, and squirts for me . . .
Mouth open wide, but no sound . . .
A silent scream . . .
Collapsing out of position . . .
Heavy breathing spastic twitching . . .
Fluttering eyes rolling back . . .

Deep voice, a soft whisper . . . "Shhh . . . she's still talking to me."

Mirrors:
Let Us Watch Us

Black bodies under moonlight glow
Perspiration lost in sexual meditation
Silhouettes entwined in erotic reflections
Twisted we are contorted figure eight positions
Admiring our window display

Entering your bliss
Watching you watch me
Taking pleasure in the motion picture
Slow motion wind, voodoo in my hips
Erotic musical renditions of my stroke

Multiple orgasms in third person
Screaming to me, visually we encourage you
Talking to yourself, in sexual conversation
Squirting on three-dimensional tongues in one
Identical orgasmic twins of mirror sexual images

Embedded nails scratch at the floor
Eye to eye with you, talking to yourself
Multiple arguments with multiple orgasms
I make your body talk to me
As you scream at you

Sexsensual

Bilingual lips and trilingual tongues
In her language sweetly she comes
Bodies vibrating in orgasmic duets
Simultaneously you bite your lips
Watching as she bites her lips

Straddle my hips
Watch yourself, tease yourself
Seduce your g-spot, find your rhythm
Orchestrate your sensual choir
Sing your song, dance with yourself

Scream in octaves
Cream in soprano
Squirt in bass
Orchestrate your hips
Write your music on my face

Erotic personas
Split personalities
Jazz in sexual nirvana
Admiring our assorted faces
Mystic mirror images of ecstasy
Mannequins that move life-like in moonlight
Dancing with ourselves we are out of body realities

Scream

Vibrating vocal cords
Bodies on one accord
Abstract twisted positions
Black sweat in blue moonlight
Silhouettes of love's interpretations
Orgasms howling, crying into the night

Night rider, ride me in reverse
Suckling lips, your mouth my curse
Slap my body with yours once more
Kinky extractions suck the voice out me
My shadow must follow
Yet secretly envy me

Jealous hard-on from Father Time
Seven-thirty pounding passion into time
Sign-language hieroglyphics, tracing figures in the air
Seven orgasms past ecstasy, bodies that wind past nine
French kissing ocean rushes savoring, you swallowing mine

B.O.B:

Battery-Operated Boyfriend

Mechanically sound, brown sculpted back
Black flesh-tone, personally ordered to please
Stamped: Personal freak
Aiming to please, erotic battery
With a life time warranty

Equipped with snake-like motion
Thick joystick, impulsive artless art
With unusual twisting of my tongue
Vibrator between your hips
Looking to turn you out

Slow to fast, all the in-between
Convertible from the top
Transformable to the back
Cruise control to make
Your eyes roll back

The drizzle of your cream
My lips your dream
The vibrator to your clit
As I savor kissing your lips
You lose it

Legs quiver lying in a daze
Too weak to walk
Too exhausted to talk
Body in withdrawal
I am your sexual twelve step relapse

Hold that pose on your knees
Built with no on or off switch
Made to stroke you feverishly
Hands grip the small of your back
Animated moans and ass claps
Orgasm too strong to fake
Questioning your legs endurance
That continuously vibrates

Forgot to check the box
For discontinued orgasm use
Delivering sex out of the box
No caution sticker on my ass cheek
For when this pleasure stops
I am built to last, I aim to please . . .
Friend to the end . . . your flesh-toned dream
Your battery-operated boyfriend . . .

Like a Real Freak

6 inch Stilettos on candy feet
Sleek legs chocolate glazed
A body with more curves
Than the smoke of purple haze

She sits back on the couch.
She grips my chin, in control no doubt
Heels propped on the mirror coffee table
Bound hands, only my mouth is able
Tracing her lips glazed with gloss.
A finger signaling me to come here . . .

Following her instructions.
So out of control with her in control.
She grips my baldhead tight.
"I'm in charge tonight"
She smears my face against her lace
With a stern voice "No . . .
Lick my lips Through my panties baby."

Her moans are deep
"Yes please me, tease her
Slow down . . . it's all about me."
Tasting her through her lace
Writing pleasure on her face

My tongue to her lips.
Glazed face juice, nectar spills
Sexually dehydrated, thirst filled
The sweet taste, I take pleasure
Lapping at black pearl treasure
"Stop lay back, I run this place".
Seductively straddling, chain rattling

"I want to ride your face".

Grinding friction
Feeding my addiction
Down my chin juice trickling,
Cupping my head, as I gazed up
Drinking from her cup
Swimming below her waist
Enticing licks she's fighting,
Wetness increasing, heat rising.
Cat scratching, muscles contracting
Smothering my face, at an uncontrollable pace

"I tamed you well"
"Conditioned you to make me yell"
I slide her to the edge of the couch
Gliding my lips from her Stiletto
To her pedicured toes

Panties to the side, my tongue deep inside
Her honey pot reacts, and releases . . .
My tongue it squeezes, eyes roll back in bliss
A slave to the below the waste kiss . . .

Sometimes . . . They Like It Rough

Switch it up, rough with it
Skirt up
Panties to the side, tongue inside
Back against the wall, pelvic tilt
Ass up

Tasting love, drink it
Slurp and suck, unrestricted
Scream my name, cream on my stroke
Deep throat, soft choke

Boots planted, naked sweaty rough
High-speed ecstasy, orgasmic sign language
Cumming a foreign tongue
"Fais má parle ton chanton"
English to French
"Make your kitten talk to me . . ."

Embrace it, be lost in it
Don't run from it, pleasure to pain
Wrap your legs around it, climax unconscious on it
Invading deep internal, external rhythmical pounding
Digging nails gripping paint, on blurry halls
Pressing into clapping ass of sugar waterfalls
Weak kneed sliding down the wall

Thick cream muffled screams
High temperature bodies in black sweat
In unison, back in motion to hips in rotation
Gasping air, inhaling another orgasm
Legs viciously shaking, toes like balled fist
Orgasm onset, stroke it, until you pass out
Vibrating body, sex-quaking until she pulsates
Electrically you twitch removal of my switch . . .

Spontaneous

Impulsively, I strip
Silk panties from the back
Erotically dragging my fingers
Through her wet folds methodically
I firmly place my hand around your neck

Whispers of commands
Thickness between your cheeks
Silent pussy lips are muffled by
Sweet thrust through twitching legs
Light-headed orgasm, I embrace your neck

Pleasure to pain
Scream my name
Silently serene internally you scream
Teary eyed taking it
Convulsion thighs erupt

Collapsing in relapse
Crawling knees that vibrate
Don't run from this, take this
Orgasmic torment, sexual uplift
Drug-like strokes

Still embracing your throat
Eye contact must be maintain
Fight not to let them water
Exotic sexual highs, spaced out screams
Uncontrollable limbs flailing in the wind
Gripping nails in paint, gripping your neck

Release every bit
Of liquid sensation
Reverberation of the uninhibited
Cream deep from within, join me
In this fantasy exhibition of spontaneity

S.Q.U.I.R.T.

Spray my face with nectar
Sweet, trickling down my chin

Q uench my thirst
Clinch my tongue, as I lick her in reverse

U nwind your vocal cords
Scream and strip your throat, until verbally hoarse

I nvoke your hips until you pulsate
Rotating until your legs vibrate, kegel me continuously

R evolve your pelvis until your orgasm evolves
Speaking in tongues in the language of cum

T hrust until you cuss salivate and seethe
Clinch and release balled fist until you cease to exist

Siphoning the sap from your roots nuzzled in your bush
Humidity sticky on my lips, nectars dew

Q ueue your vocal cords to sing
Pulsating diaphragm rhythmically push and pull me away

U nintentionally you shudder, language lost you stutter
Dancing legs that flutter, my suffocating face finds breathe in you

I ronically this is tragic comedy, as you cry
With happy endings; this addiction is just the beginning

R esuscitation of your fever, I orchestrate oral addiction
Lapping you physically I control you my erotic mime

T reason in multiplicity, under my control
You squirt your allegiance to me, we scream I pledge to thee

Anonymous caller . . .

"Sorry baby I'm working
But, let me still take care of you"

Imagine me, close your eyes
Inhale my scent, lick your lips
Taste me
Remember the last time . . .

"Massage her for me . . .
Through the lace . . .
Caress your lips. . .
Picture my face. . ."

Explore your intimate, unknown erogenous zones
Breathe to my sexual rhythm; bring me there through the phone
Find my touch in yours finger tips

"Slide your panties off. . .
Where's your artificial me?
Vibrate your pearl like it was me. . .
Relax let your mind run. . .
Imagine my tongue. . ."

Trace your entrance, with shallow strokes
Tease her drizzly wet, until she spills sap
Between soft round cheeks

"Slowly insert me deep. . .
"Wind your hips slowly. . .
Raise your legs. . .
Pull your knees back. . .
Rotate your hips. . .

Grind on your artificial me"

Deep breathing, grinding teeth
Remembering me, pulsate to my stroke
Sweetly let yourself go

"Increase the pace. . .
Squeeze him like he is me. . .
I know she so wet wanting me. . .
I here her talking through the phone. . ."

As she pulsates, slow your pace
Hold your climax, don't let it go
Squeeze me tight, I want your bed soaked

"Listen close. . .
Answer your bedroom door. . .
But stay on the phone. . .
Don't be scared of the shadow. . .
I want you in person, but on the phone . . .
Stroking you from the back, listening to your moans. . .
Your lips competing for the phone. . .
You climax. . .
Now open the door for me. . .
I'm on the other side . . ."

To be continued . . .

The Right to Cry

I hereby give you
Saturated nonverbal communication
Secreted from your lips and eyes
In this syndication to scream on this channel

Your sheets will be sexual tissue
You and she will both be issued
A sexual amendment, an erotic revision
Multiple articles of orgasm and revised climax

Scratch this moment on the floor
You will cum until vision is blurred
Take this sexual nervous breakdown
Of constitutional right of uncivilized nights

You have been given
The right to scream erotic bylaws
This is the action of a lost amendment
From the erotic Articles of Cum-fession

All this wetness
There is no recession
Only Fourth of July water-works
The independence of sexual sovereignty

I hereby
Reinstate you the *Sexsensual* right
To relentlessly hold me tight and fight me
Until you bite the bed sheets, it is however ok
To exercise the right to cry . . .

Thug Love

Sorry if I'm indecisive
Multiple positions, meet my alter ego
The flat of my tongue I drag
From front to back

Naked body, fitted hat to the back
Sexual beast, boots on my feet, I stroke to the beat
Gangsta music pumps to my pound
Subwoofer moans, amplified groans

I ambush the puss
Ripped Victoria into strips
Throw your body to the bed
Stick my face in the bush, to make you shush

My gentleman is sleep
Meet the rough and raw in me
Mattress sliding to floor
Neighbors knock at the door

Cush blows with my push
Drenched wet lips in your afro-bush
Aphrodisiac licks, drunk off pussy juice
Black n' Mild smoke floats to my stroke

Don't run just take it, too real to fake
Let me your orgasm vandal of multiple robberies
Compulsively squirt for me

www.dot.cum

I've viewed your profile, seen your pictures
I'll admit I've changed some, rotated your pictures
Cropped your clothes off, moved your body into positions

One leg on my shoulder, another cupped in my arm
Legs wrapped around my waist, pressed bodies against the wall
Chocolate legs wrapped around my back
Teasing you with my thick tip
Some nights you chase me with your hips
Others you cream off my keys strokes
Sticky fingers invading your web cam
Typing until a hard-on hold on

Something about you riding me
The way you bounce then rock . . . rock then bounce
Gripping your ass, as I work you from the bottom
Then stop

Change positions as you squat and frog hop
You type the visual ***{HOT CAN'T STOP CUMMING!!!}***
My eyes locked on your web-cam, staring with a confused face
I can't help but think
"Dayumm what a wonderful sex face
She's creaming all over the place"

I wanna turn you out . . . do the unthinkable
Trace erotic html code on sugar walls
To the sound of you losing it
Ass biting the bed sheets
Thick thighs compressing my face
Spastic contractions, drenched and wet

Body twitching, rhythmic contortions
Silver Bullet vibrating clit
Orgasmic energy vibrating your hips
My tongue slurping your lips
Placing the toy in my mouth
Continue down south

A wicked combination no doubt
Losing control minutes past creaming
Body switching gear
From creaming to squirting
You type ***{WTF!!!}***
Connection lost
Digital WET DREAM signing-off

Pussy Control

It is unacceptable
What you are capable
Of doing to me

In your lips you vehemently
Suck me with strangle hold
Clinch my stick
Enfolding my thickness

Take my mind
Mayor of my body
I elect your sexual femininity
Coarse voice I scream pussy control

Electric chair therapy
As she straps me down
Psychologically she shakes me
Straitjacket holds that don't let go
Overdosing me with pussy control

Squat in your heels
Ride me until I am hoarse
Lock my body up in your gates
Slapping my face bristly, take my voice
My masculinity screams out of control
For your pussy control

She Den' Worked A Root

What did she put on me?
That had me cussing in tongues
Curling my toes until I forgot my own name
She had to have that majestic sugar cane
I'm stuck in withdrawal, she was Miss Black Cocaine
Voices saying from draws to balls
I rule you

Was it what I licked?
Steady walking into love's potholes
Why am I in this pussy predicament?
I can't feel my legs, stalking my own shadow
As she walks by with him and winks with sly sentiment
I'm in the mirror in the dark arguing over the nightmare with myself

I remember lovin' so well
I know it got roots in it
She walked my dog with no legs
She had me high with no head
Now I'm hearing voices
Trying to scratch her image out of my head
She had to put that Marie Laveau hoodoo
I control what you do on me
I'm talking about that chocolate alley cat
Had me barkin' marriage vows out loud

Is this my demise?
I'm trapped in a web with thick legs
Fighting my own bed-sheets

It's like I lost my mind
Walking forward to counter clockwise time
Put on my best tie with no shirt
My belt and dress shoes with no pants I'm going to church

But she's magical even
I'm naked and running in love
Going nowhere fast
I swear I can't wait to get to church
Get a little sanctified that can't hurt
I just need to find my mind first

Guilty

Don't run from this sentence
Tied up with mental restraints
I give it for the memory in your life
Remember me on mundane nights, alone
This sexual sentence, moaning with jail bait strokes

You cannot acquit any part of me
Blameworthy you wrap your legs tight
Deeply appreciated sexually inebriated your court squirms
Wrapping my hands around your neck like order in my court
Slamming my gavel with authoritative jurisdiction
You scream with conviction

Don't acquit this, climax relentlessly, illicitly allow your jury
To take this in, to absorb this sexual circumstantially soaked evidence
If I pull my lips away at this moment allow me to show the court your guilt
Your significant quantity corroborating orgasmic evidence glazed on my lips
Don't appeal this, as I lick the evident nectar away
Swallowing the burden of proof

I am representing myself, as the expert witness
My own self-appointed partner in crime
Let us both be found guilty
Of this orgasmic offense of premeditated presumption
We will be repeat offenders
Our mental jurors will never leave us with a hung jury
Scream the veredictum until you come
No one will adjourn this multiple orgasm case
Addicted persons that lay covered with sweat

Unlimited uninhibited we are
With no statute of limitations

Endless nights of turning each other out
We are a hung jury of deliberation
Scratch in my back "I am guilty"
And we will still smile as we commit it again
For we are never guilty of lost love
Yet guilty and in love
We will without end
Forever live self-sentencing lives
Of due process in love forever in mistrial

MEN-age à trois

Softly you take his thick tip
Sweetly I take your vertical lips
Wind your neck, followed by your hips

Elaborate strokes, intricate slurps
The dessert you deserve, sensual we serve
Salivate, then catch your nectar, moan as we rule you

He slaps your face, I slap your cheeks
Stand on all fours, trembling hands and knees
Flipping your body, turn the page of this fantasy over

Wrap both lips around this ecstasy
Clench the climax of the moment with arched back
Chase this bliss with your hips, savor him with your lips

Swallow us with every scream
Take it, don't run from it, gush from this rush
Lose your voice, silently tears, we stroke you to a hush

L.I.C.K.

Listen to the sliding of my tongue
Invading your flower lips
Careening my lips, I dance French kiss
Kinetic rotations, pulsating, winding your hips

Labeling you mine, I trace erotic design
Inducing strokes, flicker your black pearl rain from behind
Coordinating uncontrollable convulsions of sexual reactions
Kleptomaniac, taking over, I thieve multiple orgasmic satisfactions

Lapping away your mental stability
Inversion conversion of bodily positions
Curling toes, drug induced, lost in the pillows you yell
Knocking on the walls of ecstasy's door, ringing orgasm's bell

Lifting your hips into a g-spot face sitting position
Introducing hypnotic tongue twisting, as your legs began to quake
Creamy center delight, licking you into an unconscious state
Kidnapping your breath, blindly you reach, orgasmic loss of speech

Licking hot tongue, clapping against swollen clit
Insisting you don't run, holding your
thick hips
Chasing your orgasm with my face, holding that pussy in place
Kegel my tongue, karma's a bitch as you twitch, paying the price for talking shit

Lifting legs V—stretched, orgasmic bilingual screams
Ice cubes melting from my mouth into your lip's cream
Cascading your waterfall softly on my face, you sit, I lick
Keepsakes of your nectar on my lips, squirting joy, addictively I am your fix

Lay on your stomach, with elevated cheeks and hips
Inside you quake, I am your pulsating flesh-tone vibrator
Cum laude, earning honors, begging for continuous release
Kodak moments, erotic optics, visual multiple brain clicks as I lick

Licking . . . flickering
Involuntary muscles contractions, sucking
Caressing folds of untold ecstasy's, succumbing
Keenly I remember your bodies map when I lick . . .

Gentleman Thug

I am your gentle, I am your rough
I am your tender, I am your love
I am your gentleman
I am your thug

Breakfast in bed, candlelight dinner
Oil massages, your romantic servant
We can argue, put me in my place
As I place you in yours, I am in charge of course

I am naked satisfaction, no clothes, just
Timb Boots rugged
No bed, I grind on the floor, deep n' slow
Feel all of me, I am your thug
My lips French kiss your lips, gripping your hips
I position your clit flicker, slurp, and suck

Toes curling snapping like Love Jones
Abnormal orgasms, you squirt, I slurp
Your personal freak, soft whispers of
"What are you doing to me?"

I am your gentle, I am your rough
I am your tender, I am your love
I am your gentleman
I am your thug

Sexual Hypnotism

Lay down on this couch
This is something past therapy
Psychologically spread your legs
Arch your mind up and wrap around this
Let me be your hypnotic licks, your sex theory
I am speak softly baritones that make your brain moan
Rhythmically sway this tongue side to side in pussy hypnosis
I am sweet psychoanalysis, sucking you into screaming paralysis
In your mind I am the pulsating slow grind white coat erotic stethoscope
Climb on top of me and ride, emotionally overdose come until comatose
Let me be you mind machine, your orgasmic order, cure to your disorder
Come with me in high-definition cinematic mind screams
This is mental sexual revelation in hot stress gushes
Wet limits sliding on lips squirting feedback
Slowly push back, sway back into reality
Coming out of mental hedonism
Off your finger suck this
Sexual Hypnotism

Plagiarism

In no contest I confess

Yes
I have ripped the pages from your inner most
Walls

Licked the thoughts from your mental representation, made it my own
Do

Not authorize her to speak when spoken to or prohibit her
To

Unleash paint on canvas, with squirting brushes because walls do
Talk

I steal from you, from your land of Eros

Tearing fantasy from your mind, making it mine

This is not my original work,

Yes

Walls

Do

To

Talk

Josephine

"In memory of the great Josephine Baker"

I still hear jazz in the universe
With my St. Louis girl's soul
Danced my way to stories untold
Rhythmically prancing around the globe
France still pants, holding it's breathe in awe
Paris fell in love with me, now she is black like me
She, music, and I fell in love
A musical ménage à trios

I wooed a rainbow of races
Singing to the hearts of seductive faces
I danced Africa into white hearts
Naked bananas on my hips
My banana pudding sweet on men's lips

My song, a ballad, played back
My skin too beautiful not to win
Black queen beginning to . . .
My song never ends . . .

Still swaying my hips in the wind
Singing acoustics in heaven's breeze
Congo drums in my blood
I danced atop a tightrope
Atop heaven's gates, as angels blushed
Jesus in the front row
I still hear jazz in the universe

Control Me

Unleash
Set free
Give rein to me
Hold my head under
Climax

Drink

Sapping
Come juice
Running down legs
Begging mouth satisfyingly fed
Head

Untitled

Edible
Flower mound
Black coffee cream
Take this until you scream
Delectable

This Fight

You have legged locked me in
But your orgasm I will not let go
Now you are hysterically begging me to end
No, you will forcefully enjoy my hold, ignoring your no
Cum until you slap me, scream until you bite me; mischievously I grin

Remember Me

Let the memories of this night
Dance in your head years from today
Rock with me on your porch grey haired beauty
Smiling a smile, I remember you

Wash those dishes wet
See my reflection of sweet confections
Inhale my scent and taste the recollections

Whistle that tune, moan those blues
That rocked your thighs, with sweet soul
Remember the poetry of a poem that was physically written

In This Moment

In this moment, hear me when I say
I need to love you now, to breathe you now
Take my life in this hour, can't you see death is near

Miss Sweetness ladylove
Take my hand be my life support
Release this heavenly soulful thing in me
I need your heartbeat, pump this thing in me

Make love to me, don't let me go
Guide this blind man's hand tonight
Student of human nature be love's tutor
My last piece of bliss, take my last good kiss

Stubborn man, up until now
Paralysis in my hips, body in a crypt
Lady-love groove this soul, I'm not too old
Sanctified lady let me show you what you mean to me

In this moment, hear me when I say
I need to love you now, to breathe you now
Take my life in this hour, can't you see death is near?

Sonnet 69

She is the sweetest weakness
I savor her wet honey pot
I drink her nectar, I need this
Dwelling tongue in walls hot

He is my thick confection long
Pretty girthed love song, rhythm stick
Mounting him, I sing my longest song
Taking him deep, his eyes watered, time didn't tick

Dual therapist, physiologically erotica entwine
I savor delectably pulsating stream
Great minds tangled as one, sexually we are our own kind
He drinks my spouting convulsing cream
She is my body, he is my mind, we are six lives past nine
He is my body, she is my mind, we are six lives past nine

Woman No Cry

Poor woman, no cry

Blind women, no see
This dance, I will lead
Controlled erotically, by me
Screaming woman, don't cease;
Deep abyss woman, drown me at sea
My lips will continue to forever pacify
Wipe the tears from between your thigh
Dreaming woman, this is an out of body reality

Drinking Rain

Tasting nectar tangy
Vertical lips rain
I drank
My thirst rises again

Hearts In Love

Distant we grow
He was never me
Seeds of love we sow
She was never you
Years of tears that won't let go
Separated souls left home
Destined hearts that can't let go
Nowhere, did we really go

Cheater's Moment

We lie and stare gazing deep
Holding this moment we cannot be
We love as we weep kissing

Wine

I like my pussy with wine
Poured over lips I lick
I like mine dripping from the vine

With Care

My tongue brushes through hair
Perpendicular wet walls
Fingers brush through my hair

Erotica Jazzing Me

Tantalizing Africa in her hips
Sweet leg music in chocolate variation
We are our own beat in horizontal syncopation
Black rhythms dripping hymns, naked bodies on no names
streets Progressive percussion banging hot bodies cussing of
rock and roll
Back alley blues deep in thighs I hold, bodies playing on an
unstressed beat
Sixty-nine sonnets of jazz, scatting on the down strokes, scream
on the up beats
Sweet back beats, suspension of speech, on suspended beats
Oh the feeling of erotica jazzing me blue

Broken Heart Obsession

Insanely
I can't scratch you
Out of my itching head
I wrestle with your ghost
You sleep with me
Like banshees fighting bed sheets
As if my head is your bed as I awake it's just me

I walk and smile, like you don't exist
Trying cut your love out me
So that I may exist
Release a piece of me

I sleep with the ghost of you
Many women I've tried on
Hoping to replace you
Yet there is no equal
Seemly you wrote
My prequel

My new love, I shame her
Unable to love her
My life seems to have no sequel
You have stolen the pages to my new chapter
And plagiarized my mind from our time
Why did you make love to me this time?

Why do you smile?

Like you own a million of my nights
Give my love her face back
Her smile back, her effervescent essence
So I may inhale her and enjoy her scent
Hear her voice in sentences
It is her I want to see
When she sleeps
Why are you still looking at me?

Love's Serenity

Forever is not long enough
As I asked God for another lifetime
To love you in angles
That love you right

I want to love you into a place
Called the epiphany of serenity's insanity
Spend the longevity of nine lives of my life loving you right
The Angel of Tranquility, marrying my zodiac, the lion in me
King of Love

I stole the book of God's Romance
To love you right, pearly gates that open upon high
Secret gardens with Eden's kisses and fruit edible from
trees to please
I savor a romance that dances soliloquies seven years worth of
love's time
Twenty-one lives in love divided by three lifetimes
The infinity equivalent of seven souls going to heaven
seven times

As I love you in a time of revelation of secret angles of sensuality
You love me in place, we exist in a space, inconsistent with a
place
Sweetly we live a life, past the arms of reality, and Father Time's
pouring sands
We are angels that forfeit their wings to fly, for love and time
To remain together forever in serenity

Love's Lost Lyrics

Lips of joy I kiss no more
Pokerfaced souls on an empty dance floor
Soliloquy of lost lips, she sings my song no more
Dancing tunes, on his broken notes, my music falsely written by he
Smiling in one-way mirrors romantic reflections, floating on his sea
Pride please release me, so she may see, I am love, and she is me
Have not I learned, the lessons, the teachings
Blindly reading, written brail, the book of love's preaching's
Love scriptures singing, I naively play backwards, sightlessly reaching
Sermonize my wondering soul, intangibly her blues are unmanageable
I long at night, craving her touch, tasting her in my sleep she is delectable
My internal court adjourns, an emotional recess, the personal postpone of romance is inevitable
Forever I will yearn, in my internal abyss, journeying for her, a piece of heaven through life I will explore.
Nothing more than a soulless mannequin's worlds apart, may I find, so I may again aspire to be
The essence of what was before I lost love, maybe in heaven we can be heaven's duet, her and me
I hunger for my fill, until then my appetite for life is sourly inedible

The Other Man:
Her Letter of Addiction

When we make love
She tells me
Whispers in my ear

"I can't release you, not even in my sleep
Sadly, I make love to my love, while riding waves of you"

"In my storm with you, sadistically I smile in a place of peace,
In love
Deeper than the breath that feeds me I try to let this go
In hopes of finding my sanity
It's like insanity is making love to vanity
Birthing a narcissistic love-child
Named destiny
My conscious won't forgive me, involuntarily my body
Makes love to night air, I pull my own hair
When you are not there
Running while I sleep, away from you I curse you,
I hate you
Coming
I'm coming
And I swear, I can't take you"

She says she can't shake me, not even in her dreams
Now she chooses not sleep, to try and defeat
This romantic anomaly, erotic sexual hyperbole
That drenches her sensually wrenches
From her brain to her feet
Commonly known as me

"You intensify my senses
Become my lungs
I inhale deeper to breathe you
Afraid to exhale
I spray your cologne when I am alone
Worried that I might lose the essence of you
Suffocating myself to keep you
I hold my breath
Even your shadow
I am beginning to envy
Oh, how I love a piece of you in me."

If you are wondering exactly
How she became to be in this mental state I must say and happily admit
I only dated her mind
Massaged her cerebrally to succumb
Running with nothing but her mind running wild
She comes to me, then she comes on me
In this physical form pre-conformed
Mentally self-seduced
With pre-come
In multiple sums

"Uncontrollably, I can't unwrap my mind
A naivety that dismisses dreams that we can't be
Mightily I try to release my legs from around him
I am in love with a love that consumes my day

Mentally molesting my nights into wet bliss
And multiple soul kisses"

Vehemently she wants to unplug me
So her lips say
Yet she has locked me in her reason
With constituted sexual by-laws
Exercising her first sexual amendment
Against her erotic prohibition
Uninhibitedly she screams

"Yes, yes, No, let me go
You feel so right, right there
I'm... coming...I'm...not...running...I'm...coming
I can't feel my body
I see my body vibrating I feel so out of body"

The rest is wet run-on sentences furthering
Her self-sentencing repentance
As I lick my way to remittance
She says it is her orgasmic constitutional right to me
By any means legal or illegal I have jurisdiction
If she turned my reality off
In her dream surely she would cream
In daydream

"I confess he is the epitome
That won't allow me home
He is twilight torture
I'm addicted
To tomorrow . . ."

Excerpts from Sexsensual: Chokolate

Book 2

of the

Sexsensual Trilogy

Erotic Short Stories
&
Select Poetry

Ghetto Love
(Erotic poem & Short Story)

Tired of arguing
The fussing and fighting
Passion eclipses the dysfunctional
Psychological sexual therapy, the cure

Heated attitudes, nose to nose
The slow removal of our clothes
Echoes of past screams directed at me
Your fingers, once disgusted, in my face
Randomly my lips trace, sensually taste
Easing the tension floating around
Leisurely, I go down

Slowly, you wrap your legs around me
I grind slow; you squeeze and pull me in deep
Apologetic lips conversing, lost in passionate sorrow
Drenched thighs accepting my every sorry
Multi-orgasmic amnesia, memory lost
What was it we argued about?

Frozen in the moment we stare,
Love and hate
Pain and tears
I am you
You are me
We are one
Intensely we soul kiss

Glistening in sweat
My stomach to your back
One leg cupped in my arm
Deep arches and intense strokes
High off your drug
Moans I release
Our problems up in smoke

Inhale exhale in search of sex highs
The edge of the bed
Looking over your shoulder
You wind and back it up slow
Your hair locked in my hand
Sensual aggression pulling about
The singing of sexual ass claps
I hold my own, stand my ground

Softly you whisper
"I'm about to mmm"
The gritting of your teeth
Biting bed sheets
Arched back raining cream
Your nails that grip so tight you remove sheets
Reaching for shit that don't exist
You scream out
No sound comes out

You collapse out of position
Run from my stroke
I brace your hips
You bite your lips

I moan
"I can't take this shit."
Bodies exhausted
Tension deflates
Problems resolved
A Ghetto Love released . . .

"Ghetto Love"

"Who the fuck do you think you talking to Tia?"

Christion's voice blared with bass-filled anger. He stood with jean shorts, wheat-colored Timberland boots on, and his black, fitted Pirates hat tilted to the side. His white t-shirt was off, tucked halfway into his back pocket. The platinum "T" emblem, for Tia, on his chain, stuck to the left side of his chest. Christion was well built and cut from all the weight lifting he did and his roofing jobs. The deep chocolate tone of his body, and precision cuts, seemed almost etched into his still half-sweaty body.

"I've been outside working on the damn house and you come home yelling and shit. In the yard causing a scene. The neighbors watching and you trippin'."

"Fuck them!" Tia screamed.

"Are you Christion? You are cheatin' on me? I knew it!" Tia shouted pointing her finger directly into his forehead pushing. Throwing her red and gold Coach bag on the black leather sofa, as her red spaghetti strapped sundress flared up, as she tried to march past him.

"What are you talking about? I'm not cheating on you T; I love you, what the fuck?" Christion's tone was calm, as he grabbed her arm to slow her down.

He may have well been cheating on her, with all the overtime he had been putting in. But he hadn't been with anyone else.

She was his heart. Deep inside he wanted to reveal it, it was for a good cause; something he wanted and so did Tia. He just couldn't tell her, not yet.

"I found the fuckin' receipts! For the jewelry!" Tia worked her neck with her hands on her hip. "I ain't wearin' nothing new! Who's the bitch?" snatching her arm away distancing herself.

"You ain't shit! You a foul and shady nigga."

"Oh I'm a nigga now?" Christion tilted his head to the side.

She had truly touched a nerve calling him a "nigga". He despised it and believed too many black men were already labeled that.

"You betta calm yo' ass down, I know that much! Let me explain."

Tia was furious. She loved Christion ever since they met. At first, she wrote him off as some thug, a typical nigga, or another grown thirty-plus black man that saw life in white tees, with plans in life about as long as his dick was long. When she saw him talking to the Hispanics working on the roof of the house next door, she figured he should be trying to get a job like them. Christion approached her later revealing he managed them and owned the roofing company that was doing the work. He later told her to stop judging a book by its cover or she'll miss the message inside.

Christion walked up behind Tia as she walked into the kitchen. "Come here, come here you trippin'." He tried to pull her arm, firmly but gently, to slow her down.

Whomp!

"I hate you! Fuck you Christion!"

The echo of Tia's slap was heard throughout the kitchen. The sound cut through the silence of the room. The pause was long. Their breathing was audible. The music playing in the other room was now empty background noise, unfitting for the mood.

"Have you lost yo' gawt damn mind?" Christion yelled, grabbing her by both shoulders firmly.

Tia flinched and shut her eyes tight. She knew the slap or punch was coming . Fist or hand was on its way to knock her out . It never came . Instead he kissed her resolutely. He sucked her bottom lip into his mouth. Tia's fear stayed; the kiss confused her. She was trembling. She hit him and he kissed her? Her thighs quivered, her pussy pulsated with anxiety and trepidation. The confusion puzzled every part of her in that moment. Christion kissed her with more passion. Then he ripped the spaghetti straps of her red sundress. Then he ripped off her black strapless bra. He stared at her so intensely she had to look without breaking eye contact. She was paralyzed by the actions in this intense moment. He walked her body back to the light blue wall next to the entrance of the kitchen. Her heels and his boots were loud on the hardwood floors.

Christion was clearly pissed. He looked threatening and serious. He towered over Tia at six foot three; she was only five foot four. Her heart trembled with fear. She had crossed the line.

"So you gon' just slap me huh, well I'ma punish that ass and you gonna love it." It was a stern, yet seductive voice.

Tia moaned as her anger was now transformed into sticky wet madness that dripped soppy wet on Christion's hard-on.

Christion invoked fear again in Tia slapping her ass maliciously, her cheeks wavered. The burn of the slap welted her behind. “Ahhhh.” Tia winced.

“Shut . . . the fuck . . . up.” Christion said plopping Tia’s hard nipple out of his mouth. He pushed her hard against the wall.

Tia’s heart raced. These feelings of fear, confusion, passion and the fury in her pussy confused her. She could’ve moved or stopped if she wanted to. She came intensely, purely off the power of the moment. Her body shook vehemently.

“Christion why are you . . .”

“Shut the fuck up.”

Tia had no response and she was not in control. She was a prisoner and guilty. She was sentenced to all she felt: fear, sexual tension, anger, and confusion.

Christion pushed her off his dick against the wall daring her naked body to move as he descended to his knees. He got up close to her pulsating vertical lips and made no eye contact with her face, he stared at her pussy. He grazed his nose against her clit. He breathed slowly into them, inhaling her. “This my pussy”, he said as he stared angrily up at Tia, then buried his face into her pussy to satisfy his anger.

“Oh my god,” Tia said in fear and wonder.

Christion slurped at her pussy, as if he was using his tongue to sexually whip and sensually torment her with punishment. He would stop short of her climax and then began again repeatedly. As if he was searching for an orgasm that was lost deep inside her. As if the one coming would suffice or justify his mission. He flicked her engorged clit and breathed her juice into his mouth and nose. The loud French kisses of his lips and her pussy could be heard in the kitchen. Tia gripped his shoulder with one hand the wall with the other. She clawed both intensely.

"Oh god, oh god, oh god, oh god!" Tia grunted. Her voice and tones made her nervous, out-of-body sounds. "Ohhh ohhhh, oh god." She heard herself coming in stereo.

Both of Tia's legs vibrated on Christion's shoulders. Tia gritted her teeth and squirted. Tia bucked against the immovable force, Christion didn't budge. She was trapped between the wall and the powerful orgasms. He was strong and never lost her. His moans were angry and hungry. Tia was airborne and couldn't run from the sensation; elevated back against the wall and her legs wrapped tightly around his neck.

She pleaded "Please, please, I can't take it baby."

Christion ignored her and gripped her ass harder holding her in place as her red sun-dress draped over his head.

"Fuck, oh no, oh no," she released warm tangy fluid into Christion's soppy, glazed mouth again.

Tia wrapped her legs tight around Christion's neck, still elevated on his shoulders against the wall, to momentarily catch her breath and to stop him. He worked quickly at the zipper on his jean shorts and pulled them down using his feet to kick them off. He lowered Tia down and pushed her by both shoulders to her knees. The force was enough to let her know she had no choice.

"Put this deep in ya' mouth." The soft confident tone was smooth from his lips. Tia grabbed the base of his iron-hard manhood. Christion knocked her hands away.

"Use your mouth, no hands. You touch it again, I'm a slap

you." Tia's pussy was dripping as she took the tip of his head in her mouth. Her mouth was wet, she drooled as she leaned forward elongating her neck as he pushed forward.

"Ummm stay deep down on it," Christion moaned, standing naked with the exception of his black fitted Pirates hat, the platinum "T" emblem for Tia on his chain and wheat-colored Timbs.

The slurping and moaning was loud and unadulterated echoing through the house. Tia began to slurp and suck with passion and apologetic moans. Her eyes watered at the depth. She looked up into his eyes, as he looked down intensely at her. She only backed off to breathe, and then hungrily engulfed Christion like she needed him in her mouth to stay alive. Christion with staggered legs flexed his muscles gripping the back of her head and began to pump his hips into her mouth as she gagged and took it.

Tia moaned and began to scream lost in the moment she came. Unaware of the zone she had put herself in, the mind state of passion, so deep she creamed from the oral pleasure she was giving. She moaned with Christion deep in her throat, the vibrations intensified as he pushed her away.

"No you can't make me come. You don't deserve it."

"Give it to me." Tia reached with her hand for more panting.

Christion raised his hand in defiance staring methodically.

"No." He pushed her head away.

"Give it . . . please give it to me."

Christion pointed his finger at her to silence her. He held it there in the air like a sword. Tia shut her voice off mid-sentence and stared like a child scolded.

“Get on your knees and turn around. Face the other way and don’t look at me.”

Tia looked, and then turned around, lifting her dress with one hand looking over her shoulder waiting for the thick dangling hard pleasure staring at her. Christion pointed his index finger for her to turn around and look forward.

“Don’t look at me.”

He towered over her. Looking down at Tia’s full, dark, honey brown ass and tiny waist made him yearn. Her red, Dolce & Gabbana, open-toed heels; graced her lovely honey brown legs. Christion stroked his dick. Her lips were thick and protruding out from between her ass. Slightly open and coated with sticky nectar from her self-inflicted orgasm. He smacked her left ass cheek hard and watched it jiggle and settle back in place.

She was his ecstasy, his erotic metaphor for love and passion. Pleasing her even in conflict was his fulfillment of pleasure.

“Please baby she is aching for you please.” Tia lay with her chest flat to hardwood floor and ass arched high serving it up. She glided her acrylic French tips through her wet sticky nectar playing in her pond. Her vertical lips glowered in waiting.

Christion knelt over her dripping wetness. He dragged his tip and moved it away whenever she pushed back for his penetration. He plunged slowly in holding it deep. Tia crossed her high heels as he filled her. Christion gripped her neck with his large hand firmly and whispered.

"Me and him have been nice far too long." He pushed his dick in deep. Tia groaned. "We don't like your attitude." He gave her more as she moaned with a squeal and her pussy tighten around him. "He doesn't want to be in your wet tight pussy right now."

Christion pulled out slowly still gripping Tia's neck enough to let her know she still had no say-so. She grinded her throbbing lips against him for more. Christion slid back in again. He put his other hand her waist and massaged her clit and began stroking her.

"Ummm" Tia moaned.

Christion increased the pace. He thrust harder with each stroke. The clapping of their skin was loud, vicious and methodical. Tia screamed at the pleasure and pain. Christion's grip tightened slightly around her neck. Tia held her breath trying to brace herself internally as her orgasm rushed to the edge of her body. The intensity of the moment, the passion, and the power of Chrsition's powerful stroke broke Tia down. The tears turned to sex cries.

"Fuck me. Please fuck me," she bucked back and cried.

"Fuck me, me, me . " Dark colored tears streamed her face from her mascara. She never finished her sentence. She was lost in the powerful rhythm of Christion's thunderous stroke, as she clinched and released him. The slushy sound of her pussy was a testament to the multiple orgasms that were induced.

"Take this dick. Take it!" Christion grunted in concentration. "Don't run." Tia tried to crawl away from the clutch of another orgasm. "You gon' keep your hands to yourself, huh?"

Tia nodded her head, emphatically. "Yes, yes, yes, my hands, to myself," she moaned and came again swallowing her complete sentence.

Christion shook, as he felt his climax; no longer able to battle the oral sex Tia's pussy performed on him.

"Ahh . . . ahhh . . ." he moaned as he pulled out leaning back toward the ceiling on his knees stroking his manhood to peak.

Tia's mouth was still hungry she quickly spun around and engulfed Christion's dick deep. She slurped until the tangy sweet fluid gushed to the back of her throat.

"Oh ma . . ." Christion moaned. "Fuck baby." His eyes rolled back. Moaning, Tia sucked until it was she who was in control and it was him trying to get away, as she chased him with her mouth. Tia sucked and took the warm gush with large swallows of apologetic satisfaction.

They both collapsed on the hardwood floor both twitching and breathing deep. They were high and euphoric in the moment. They didn't say much just laid there naked on the kitchen floor and fell asleep there.

Tia, still naked on the floor, woke-up to the clanging of a pan. Christion was preparing some dinner. He was back in his jean shorts and boots.

"You good now little momma?"

Tia nodded getting up she walked over and wrapped her arms around Christion from behind with her head resting on the side of his back.

"I'm sorry. I'm sorry I put my hands on you baby," Tia sighed.

Christion turned around and placed his finger over her lips. "We're fine and I'm not going anywhere?" He smiled. "I haven't gone anywhere."

"What about the receipts?" Tia asked innocently.

"Let's take a shower baby. Food will be done in a while." Christion just smiled and shook his head.

Christion thought and smiled to himself, "Maybe she'll notice the 2-carat ring on her ring finger, when her head clears or when we get in the shower."

Mind Me
(Erotic poem & Short Story)

Truly I will rule you
You've been so unruly
Sweetly chastise the misbehaved
Across hot cheeks my thickness slides

Strokes of submission
This will be sexual regulation
Ignoring your tap out, pass-out
You will not come until signaled by me

Wrap your legs
I grip your neck
Orgasmic tears, poor pussy
Don't cry, you will sob tonight
Erupting only when your lost body
Can find its lost mind meeting atop orgasms peak

Erotica's walking orgasm of oral education
I am the correction of sexual miseducation
Teacher of sensuality, this won't be a lesson of reality
Gripping discipline stick, you will mind me with screaming obedience

Now remove all your clothes
We will now reenact the talks of tonight
That was just a mental erotic stage play
Simple minded sexual lost student with unruly pussy
Tonight you will be tamed tonight, you will mind me

"Mind Me"

"Mmmm . . . mmm" the startled muffled sounds of desperation were partly muted from Karice's gagged mouth.

The footsteps were loud and acoustic in the room as she lay with her hands tied. The cool breeze from an open window could be felt drifting across her nude body. Her nipples were submissively erect from the chill of the wind. The room was dark, except for the glow of the streetlights, and the moonlight, casting a grayish silver radiance glow throughout the room. The sound of traffic and occasional car horns could be heard in the distance.

"Tonight is the night Karice. I've asked you, to not try and evade me. I will discipline you tonight. You will enjoy this against your own will," he said in a deep baritone voice, from across the dark room.

She began to tremble at the thoughts that began to race through her mind. *Was this the end? Would she be the five o'clock news?* She began to fight the restraints for an escape; the straps were tight around her ankles and wrist. Her body was bound and her fighting was useless.

"Stop! Stop, Karice there is nowhere to run," the baritone voice stated. The footsteps inched closer to her into the light. The dark silhouette stopped short of revealing himself in entirety, giving only the appearance of a well-built muscular baldhead man with defined sturdy legs. He was around five foot ten. His breathing was steady and calm. The brown manhood was lengthy and thick in girth dangling half angled to the right. The eye-catching sight momentarily distracted Karice's eyes. He licked his lips while rubbing his hands together.

"I know you are wondering who I am and what I want. Karice you've been bad to yourself. And I am, well, your sexual regulation." He walked out of the shadows with strong defined cheekbones, full lips, and broad naturally arched eyebrows. The man's skin was porcelain black, so dark the darkness combated his skin color. He was erotic. He was exotic.

Karice's body grew limp. Her eyes were steady. In this fearful moment she found calmness, a piece of unexplainable stillness. She gazed at his face, at his palatable length and girth, at his strapping defined legs, then reverted back to his stern face. He was not intimidating, but there was no underestimation of the power he possessed.

"You've fantasized about me . I am simply him . " Walking closer he hovered over her body at the foot of the bed, which was covered in black satin sheets. Her heart raced with anxiety. Her thighs were slick and wet with sweat. The room itself was humid, her body heat rose, and a thick moistness was mounting its arrival between her vertical lips.

She almost closed her eyes and quickly redirected her eyes to his approaching hands. She followed his hands against the rise and fall of her body. Her body was shaking. They glided across her pedicured feet. They were warm and large as he grasped her right foot lifting it to his mouth. He methodically savored each of her toes smallest to largest and back. The man's eyes never left hers as he savored her feet. A savory groan escaped his lips. Slowly he engulfed all of her toes of her size seven-foot at once. Karice's low muffled moans were of embarrassment, uncertainty and of pleasure. She couldn't resist the erogenous zone his mouth had created through her feet. The electricity of pleasure trickled throughout her entire body. Karice watched with almost passionate eyes. She was unaware of the thick cream that began flowing from within her pulsating lips, between her thighs.

"You've been so unruly in denying me every night," he said releasing her foot and licking his lips. "You hide from me. You hide from yourself—imprisoning the both of us."

He crawled up beside her. Karice was face to face with his body kneeling next to her. Her heart raced at a relentless pace. Her breast rose and fell repeatedly. He untied her hands bound with black lace underwear panties.

"If I untie you will you free yourself?" he stared awaiting an answer. "When I untie you, don't run from me this time."

Karice slowly shook her head in an obeying manner; she was not brave enough to move and try to escape. A part of her wanted to flee, and a deeper part wanted to stay. He took her hand.

"Calm down." He placed his thickness in her hands. Karice held it, her hand shaking. "It's yours, it's been yours. How does it feel? Stroke it."

Karice paused looking up at the uncompromising brown eyes. His eyes told her this was not a request but a demand. Karice began softly stroking his large manhood. His head was large and smooth. He felt hot and ridged. She could not fully embrace his thickness. Secretly Karice salivated from her gagged mouth, soaking the underwear that bound her mouth.

"He will be your discipline stick tonight. You have no control over what I will do to you, none." He removed her hand and took his hot dick and slid it across her cheeks and lips. She momentarily closed her eyes.

His body heat warmed her cheek. Karice's vertical lips twitched with sensation and hunger.

"You have been so wrong to yourself," he said tracing his manhood back and forth. "I will correct this, this sexual miseducation. You will never forget me. I will forever be accessible. I am your sexual necessity."

This man, his words, his physical being and the unknown

entranced Karice. She simply nodded as he spoke.

"You won't scream. I will remove your panties from your mouth." He took off the red lace panties that bound her mouth.

He stared at her. Karice stared back.

"Take me . . . And lose yourself." The command was calm and guiding. Karice still lying on her back leaned her head to the side. She took the tip of his thick head with her tongue into her watering mouth and clenched her thighs. Her eyes faded back, and then shut, as she sucked slowly. The traffic noise went mute. She took him deeper as saliva drizzled from the corner of her mouth. He leaned forward. He parted her thighs, pulling her legs apart and under his arms positioning himself directly over her. His warm lips sucked each vertical lip with perfect pressure. He slurped at the thick cream juice that flowed from Karice's body. She clenched her toes tight. She grabbed his hips, pulling him deeper into her throat.

"You taste like you always do," he said burying his lips and tongue hungrily into her. "You taste heavenly every night."

Karice was trying to decipher the meaning of his words, they had never met . Karice's body began to quake as he French kissed her pussy and massaged his finger into her wet ass. He pumped his large dick in and out her mouth as she slurped and screamed. She bucked and clenched her toes feverishly exploding. He stroked her pulsating ass with his middle finger and gulped the flow of the orgasmic fluids from her lips. Karice began to tap and then slap his thighs involuntarily. Scratching his body in submission, to no avail, as she exploded again having to release his dick and scream.

"Oh God, oh God, Oh my, oh ma . . ." Karice squealed and held her breath as her body lost control and erupted again. "I can't . . . I can't . . . I'm coming . . . I'm coming . . . I'm coming," she screamed!

He finally set her pussy free and positioned his body

between Karice's legs.

"This is just the beginning," he said slapping her thighs holding his inflexible dick steady. "Set yourself free Karice. And don't use your hands. Let your pussy find its way to me."

Karice complied lifting her hips up to his waiting manhood. She parted her saturated lips with his head. Karice watched her pussy slide up and down on him. Each time she licked her lips in amazement at the wet glazed icing that grew thicker with each stroke. She was finding every sweet spot she never knew she had, she came. The sopping sound of her deprived pussy clenched with satisfaction. Mentally, she was in a state of orgasm and the eruption was when her body would catch up with her mental state multiple times over.

"Turn this unruly pussy over. Fuck me until you find yourself."

Never had curse words sounded so sensual, commanding and needed. Karice rolled over on her knees, pressing her breast to the sheets, arching her ass up. She waited anxiously for him and spread her cheeks.

The presence of one stroke, subdued everything sexual she thought she knew. "Oh ma . . ." Karice gripped the sheets and came, hard. He held it deep. Leaning over her back to her ear, he didn't move directly, but with muscular control he made his dick pulsate and move inside her.

"Never deny me." He soft sucked her ear. "Never refute me. This dick or your body's need . . . for me." With each syllable he would pulsate his dick and Karice's body would shake with minor orgasmic eruptions.

He leaned up and gripped Karice's ass, parting her cheeks and stroking her pussy in methodic rhythm. The way he knew her body and controlled her orgasm, scared her. She clenched her sheets, then bit them and buried herself in orgasm—in them.

"Stop fighting me, and let go, completely go," he moaned as he gripped the back of her neck firmly. "Yes, mind me. Make this pussy mind me. It will always do what I want."

He stroke in hard staccato burst that made Karice ass clap against his skin. She was awe struck, the sound of her body's involuntary response. She gritted her teeth to the grinding sound that could be heard in her head. In sexual reflex she back bucked. She couldn't scream. The sobbing she heard in her head was her own as she cried and repeatedly spouted liquid climaxes. This out of body experience rendered her helpless. Only a face drenched with tears and sobbing could be heard.

"Please don't, don't stop. Don't ever leave don't ever take it out . . ." Karice sobbed repeatedly.

For the first time her cries brought her back to reality. She was lost in the sexual authenticity of the moment. Karice's body bucked and screamed as she fought with the sheets of her beds. Her face was drenched. She opened her eyes moaning and grabbing at her fingers lodging deeply in and out of her pussy. They pumped like hydraulics as she came and trembled staring at her ceiling fan spinning slowly.

"Oh my God! What is this?" Her body was shaking. "What am I doing?" Her bed sheets were soaked. She removed her shaking hand and fingers coated with her cum, viscous and sticky between her fingers. Fluids trickled down her wrist. She gazed at her shaking legs opening them to see her sheets also glazed with thick cum. She dropped her head back in awe. "A dream? Oh my God. A dream? Are you fucking serious?"

Her mind ran as she caught her breath. She sighed and paused. She remembered the man. His body, his voice, his words, his dick. She looked around.

"I'm going crazy."

She gasped at the sight of her red-laced panties tied in a

knot and two more black pair lying next to them.

"What is this?" She was mystified and confused. "Look at my bed, my sheets."

They looked as if they had been vandalized with water. They were wet, wild and sticky clinging to her body.

Karice laid back and recollected her dream. Clear as day in the back of her head. His voice rang out. "Karice don't ever forget me. Remember me. Mind me."

She closed her eyes; her hands roamed, and she began to mind herself.

Forever Past Heaven

(Erotic Poem and Short Story)

I shall die
Falling a million miles
If I ever dismiss my love for you

May we make moments so beautiful
We satirically cheat Father Time, with lovemaking
Pausing our reality, our creation of history

Dance the smoothest dance with me
My love, kiss me now, to savor forever later
Make love to me in repetitive ciphers of a love creation

Making love with no element of death
Let's play in the storms with smiling tears
Run with me through life a thousand more times
My our souls swim forever together as one
Let us love forever, forever past Heaven

"Forever Past Heaven"

"Please have a seat Mr. and Mrs. Hughes. I'm Doctor Larry Stanley," he said, as he took a seat adjusting his long white coat, with his glasses hanging on the tip of his nose, in perfect balance. The light glow of perspiration on his olive white forehead containing lines of concern as

he attempted to maintain a restitute poker face.

Charles took Corrine's left hand and held it tightly in his right hand. He glanced at his wedding ring taking a deep breath. Corrine's once flowing hair, that dangled freely, was now a smooth round mound of beautiful brown bald skin. Her breasts once full and supple, perfect on her modestly proportioned body, were merely low horizons containing what was left of breast. Corrine's palms were sweaty as his large brown hands palmed hers. They awaited the results. The last two months had been hard on them. The Chemotherapy treatments, the dry mouth burning sensations, the Aromatase inhibitors to block her estrogen hormones, had taken their toll on her. The inability to sometimes savor the meals that her husband cooked, sometimes unable to even hold the meal down, or to taste the cinnamon gum on his lips came and went seasonally in a moments notice.

"I'm sorry to say that the tumors have not responded to the hormone treatments or the Chemotherapy. I am truly sorry." The doctor bowed his head.

"So . . . so what's next doctor? What we got to do next?" Charles asked sitting more upright than before. As the silence set in, the dead air didn't bother to whisper a hint of positive breath.

"You're not saying nothing, so what are you saying?"

The doctor's head remained half bowed like a flag at half-staff as he wiped the sweat off his forehead, and took his wire-framed glasses off.

"She has less than four months. The cancer has continued to spread despite the treatment."

The tears streamed Corrine's face. The crying never made it to her voice. She just cried from her soul. She squeezed her husband's hand tightly, as she sat on his right side. Charles was speechless waiting for something. Anything with more time attached to it. More life to revive a hopeless grip of his wife's small hand in his.

"Naw doc. What we got to do is increase the treatment or something."

"We can't," the Doctor said.

"Why the hell not?" Charles replied as he stood up breaking Corrine's daze.

"Baby." Corrine grabbed Charles hand to calm and comfort him.

"It would surely kill her. She is already at extremely high doses," the doctor replied. "I'm truly sorry."

"That's it? That's all you can do Doc? That's all you have to say? Hell no Doc, give me something better!" His baritone voice cracked with a deep somber tone, as he cried too with no sound just a flow steady deliberate tears of pain.

"Baby calm down," Corrine said, as she squeezed his hand again that she held even as he stood. "It's not his fault. Come on let's go. Let's go figure out what we need to do."

The sound of the car hummed. Neither Charles nor Corrine said a word as they drove from John Hopkins Medical Center down the oddly empty Baltimore parkway mid-afternoon. The radio played low in the background. Charles kept his eyes on the road as Corrine gazed over at him. Charles began to sing as he drove, just as he did the first time they met, after she dared him to test his singing skills. He sang the words he sang on the night he proposed. Corrine's tears had a mind of their own as they danced down her cheeks to the melody of his deep sweet tone. Never before had she seen Charles cry. He almost cried the day he proposed. This day his own words brought tears from deep inside that poured from his eyes. He didn't blink as if he did he might miss a moment with her.

"I stand in Faith in tears, asking for years, a body pillow of compassion, soul caressing comfort . . . romance untamable". The smooth bass of his voice softly cracked and caught back up with the harmony of his soul.

Corrine reached over and squeezed her husband's thigh in comfort and rocked to his melody all the way home.

"I stand, looking with tears, into your jeweled eyes, asking for years", Charles softly blinked momentarily, closed his eyes to absorb all the love in the air. "Be my lifetime, my bonding, mate to my soul growing old, side by side".

Charles was quiet, as he ran his wife's bath water as always. The first one home would always run a steamy hot bubble bath for the other. While the other prepared dinner.

"Your bath is ready babe," Charles said, in an attentive yet bland tone with sullen eyes.

Corrine and Charles sat at the dinner table in silence and ate. The grilled Bar-B-Que salmon and steamed vegetables were hot and tempered just right. Charles sipped his Riesling and glanced up at Corrine who met his eyes.

"What are we going to do?" she asked.

"Nothing," he responded. "We're going to go on about our

lives. Live and love."

Corrine smiled. Those simple instructions gave her life and her four months began to seem like a lifetime. The security and strength of those words extended her soulfully.

Charles allowed Corrine to bathe and relax. He reflected on the day's prior events for a while, then got up to go shower. Charles showered in the separate blue granite tile shower, as Corrine relaxed in the tub. Charles stepped out the shower still wet and walked over to his wife and knelt beside the tub. Corrine was gorgeous in all her essence. Charles lovingly gazed at her. He dipped his hands into the water and ran the warm water over his wife's baldhead, massaging her scalp. Her baldhead was beautiful. The Chemotherapy, to him, did nothing to tarnish her beauty, as he kissed and washed her baldhead. Her figure was perfectly formed to his liking. He gazed at the low mounds that were where her breasts once lay; full and erect nipples once lay. Charles kissed her scars softly, licking and suckling them passionately. He bathed his wife tenderly, massaging her neck, then lathering her breast-less chest and stomach. He began caressing her legs, while she just watched and enjoy him loving her. He was her world and she was his.

They were at peace. The tears streamed her face, as he washed away her pain and the sound and thoughts of death, were at a distance.

"May I?" Charles asked, as he softly kissed her neck and ran his hand over her baldhead, with one hand and palmed her chest in the other. "Love you past forever?"

Charles took her hand and led Corrine out of the tub. The suds strolled gingerly over her curvy body. Charles stood a stout six three as he embraced Corrine that was only about five four. He squeezed her and inhaled the vanilla scented bath oil that laced Corrine's body. Charles descended to one knee and gazed up into her eyes as he hugged her waist. He lifted her leg up onto the edge of the Jacuzzi bathtub. Softly he kissed and methodically licked her leg. She softly moaned in the essence of the relaxing pleasure.

"Can we make love everyday?" "Yes."

"Like its going out of style?" he asked as his face disappeared between her legs and he softly blew on her wet clitoris.

"Yes," she moaned.

Corrine felt gorgeous. All her self-consciousness dissipated as she basked in the moment and held on to her husband's passion. Time paused.

Charles talked to every part of her body. He always managed to create an erogenous zone; she never knew she had, as he navigated her body. He knew her. He created spots where there were none and rejuvenated ones that were dormant. He softly sucked her vertical lips into his mouth, conversing with both sets of lips, seemingly simultaneously.

"You taste like summer." He licked her vertical lips softly smacking her nectar down his throat.

Corrine's body fluttered with each lick. Charles flickered then sucked her clit into his mouth repeatedly. The unequivocal repetition of tongue strokes that mastered her over the past ten years never grew bland. Corrine screamed as she gushed her warm fluid, as Charles clenched her behind and orally imprisoned her clit in his mouth. Her legs gave way as Charles lowered her down onto to red bath-rug.

"Baby I love you," Corrine said as she watched Charles gaze at her. Corrine slowly knelt and leaned forward taking Charles's thick manhood into her mouth. He moaned so deep and loud. She knew him and always re-wrote the book of his pleasure, as well. She took all of his length and girth to the back of her throat. She closed her eyes and got lost in the pleasure and the moment.

She slurped vigorously. The juices from her wet mouth, drooled over Charles pumping hips. His moan almost sounded like a song to her oral flow. Charles erupted as Corrine savored every bit of him. His body shook as he clinched the rug and arched his back into her as he knelt.

Lying in their bed Charles would watch the rise and fall of his wife's chest as she slept. Silently he cried and stole kisses from her lips, holding her, enveloping her essence and caressing her head.

They made love everyday and would fall asleep wherever they were, in that moment. Charles would paint Corrine's toes out on the patio at night as they talked and reminisced over glasses of wine and make love. Corrine would wash his feet and talk about his ugly toes. They would talk about their childhoods. How Charles never knew his father and aspired to create his own positive identity, of what a husband and a man were. Corrine would tease him about how he was a player until he met Corrine India Stephens.

She would tease saying, "Men don't think too much about love until they feel it from their balls to their bones. Then they freeze up and we have to jump their ass." And Charles knew at first sight she had both his heart and all.

Charles had enough accrued leave to take off four months with pay. He took all the leave he had. He and Corrine did everything they normally did and more. Charles and Corrine went dancing ever Friday night. Corrine loved to Salsa and Slow dance. Corrine had introduced Salsa to him on their first date. He actually caught on pretty fast. He would tease her about going on 'Dancing with the Stars' and winning. Most days, Corrine's energy was high, other days it would be low. Deep inside she would feel her body slowing down. Whenever she did, she would find strength in the love she shared with Charles. Together they stole a little more time from time. They would make love to seemly steal a little more life from death.

The quaint authentic Mexican restaurant had a very relaxed

ambiance and low lighting they slowed danced to one of their favorite songs by Carlos Santana "Love of My Life." Charles sang the sweet karaoke tune, in her ear, as they swayed side to side in unison. The pace changed as young couples flooded the floor to a Salsa fused mixed of Michael Jackson's "You Rock My World."

"Where you at baby!" Charles hit a smooth fast paced tap right, step back right, rock forward left and smooth close right taking Corrine's head.

"Whoa! Where did that move come from?" Corrine asked surprisingly responding with her own sexy Samba of a two-step. "Take you back to Africa."

Twirling, swaying, then rolling her hips Corrine dipped in and out to the musical rhythm of the chorus singing it out loud to Charles as he clapped and danced.

"You rocked my world, you know you did
(Give it to me)

(Yeah, yeah, yeah . . . yeah . . . ooh)

You rocked my world, you know you did
(You rocked my world)

You rocked my world, you rocked my world."

Charles kissed Corrine's bottom lip and softly sucked it into his mouth and released it with a smile. Twirling her body out, he broke out singing, as the crowd clapped and danced cheering them on.

Charles blared "(Come on, girl) You rocked my world (Come on, girl), you know you did (Baby, baby, baby), and everything I'm gonna give.

And there ain't nothing we could find, someone like you to call mine." Then spontaneously the Michael Jackson kick came out and Charles popped his hips moving toward Corrine. She laughed so hard, her eyes water as they hugged.

"You are a fool. Oh God, a plum fool." She said wiping tears from her eyes. "That damn Michael Jackson kick. You kick with the wrong leg."

They made it home after dancing. Corrine kicked off her red, eye-catching, patent leather, gold-tipped, peep toe, high heel Jimmy Choo's. Charles took off his dark navy blue dress shirt. Corrine was gorgeous in her matching red silk chiffon London halter dress. They made their way upstairs to their bedroom with a California king-sized bed. Charles surprised Corrine as he squeezed her from behind. He softly kissed her neck and took her elegant body into his arms and inhaled her scent. He kissed her neck and caressed her smooth baldhead with one hand and palmed her chest in the other.

"I love you baby," he whispered.

"I know you do. I am your life and you are mine. That's why we work, Charles."

Charles removed his wife's dress and let it fall to the floor and she turned around and caressed his shirtless chest. Working his pants off as they kissed, she pressed against his manhood that heated her body as it pressed against her stomach. Charles lifted her up as she wrapped her legs tightly around his waist. Her wetness drizzled and sweetly coated his stomach as they embraced. He slowly lowered her onto his erect thickness and they exhaled deeply, becoming one.

"You are me, I am you and we are one."

"Yes baby, we are. We are one." Corrine moaned and put her face in the crease of his neck.

Charles walked their joined bodies over to the bed and Corrine rolled him over onto his back. She lifted her hips slowly, and then lowered them down, as she moaned softly. Their eye contact was magnetic and time sure was at a pause with each moment of lovemaking. The tears from Corrine's face dropped on to Charles chest. Whenever they did she would lick each tear off and then kiss him.

"These are your tears." They never closed their eyes when they kissed. Charles was silent until the moment he released the tears from his soul. Corrine kissed his tears and they flowed harder. "And they are my tears." She laid her body on him and continued kissing his tears and lifting her hips as he palmed her generously round full behind, pulling her down deeper. Their breaths were steady and in sync as they listened and shared love, while their hearts beat softly pounding in one accord. Charles and Corrine climaxed in tears. Their bodies shook; never had they come so hard, so loud.

Corrine screamed and poured so much energy into love, they poured orgasmic soul into each other. No words were needed as their bodies receded into reality and then into sleep.

Charles awakened to the beam of the bright sunlight that shone extra bright into the bedroom and on to the bed. Every morning they could hear the chirping of birds outside on the bedroom balcony. That morning two Cardinals were on the windowsill as if they had been watching the whole night. Charles stared momentarily as they stared at them. The one on the right flew away. Charles then looked at his wife deep asleep, still in his arms, still pressed against his body and manhood.

"Corrine."

"Corrine baby." Her body was still. There was no rise or fall of her body. He reached for her hand. She was cold everywhere but where she was pressed against him.

"Corrine? Corrine?" Silence.

"Corrine," his voice cracked as he squeezed her tight and cried a deep soulful cry in her name.

"Sleep baby sleep."

“I’m here. I’m here.”

With his face pressed deep in her neck he sobbed holding his wife’s cool body that had passed on. He reached for her hand. It held an envelope and it read.

> *“To the love of my life you have always loved me more than me. And I have always loved you more than you. What I mean is, you were my energy and I was yours and with faith we filled each other up. I held on to you because you held me up. Charles I love you past this lifetime. You have more love to give deep in your heart. Baby you will be fine. I am always here. I return our rings, so you may one day enjoy love again. That’s how much I really love you. I am with you forever, forever past heaven.*
>
> *The Love of My Life*

The morning sunlight glared bouncing of his ringed finger. He lifted his head up slightly and recognized his ring finger had both of their rings on it. He squeezed her and broke down, his masculinity melted with endearing love and pain. He rocked his love, embracing her. He kissed her lips and whispered.

“I love you. I’ll love you forever past heaven”

Author's Note

This is a dedicated to *all* women. Especially, my women of color who have, at times, been exploited and ostracized in this unappreciative, sexist, male-driven world. We, as men, sometimes undervalue the true worth of those who bring life into this world: *women*. To my women, my black women, my women of *color*, I see you! I see your humility, your loyalty, your love, your sexuality, your sensuality and your femininity. I understand your inhibitions: your need to be *un*inhibited and those sassy alter egos of erotica hidden deep inside you. I understand you only because I have surrendered my masculinity to your femininity. And in doing so, I have come to appreciate you through my "Sexsensual eyes". I hope that, through my newfound eyes, you have journeyed to new places of creativity and openness.

To my men, my brothers of all shades and colors, let's learn to love women on new levels: more creative, self-giving levels of sex, sensuality, romance, and love. Let us set aside our egos, our *machismo*, and reveal the "King", the "Casanova", the lovers we are from within. I promise that the mental voyage you and your loved one go on will be one to last past forever.

"Love long. Love hard. Love free."
- Pharaoh Robinson

Follow Pharaoh:

Website: Sexsensual.biz

Facebook Fan Page: Pharaoh Robinson

Twitter: Pharaoh78

Big thanks to my book cover designer:

Darnell Loper

radnell66@gmail.com

Dezigns2.com

References

- Crais, Clifton and Pamela Scully (2008). Sara Baartman and the Hottentot Venus: *A Ghost Story and a Biography*. Princeton, Princeton University Press. ISBN 978-0-691-13580-9

- Fausto— Sterling, Anne (1995) . "Gender, Race, and Nation: The Comparative Anatomy of 'Hottentot' Women in Europe, 1815-1817". *In Terry, Jennifer and Jacqueline Urla* (Ed.) "Deviant Bodies: Critical Perspectives on Difference in Science and Popular Culture", 19-48. Bloomington, Indiana University Press. ISBN 0-253-32898-5.

- Gilman, Sander L. (1985). "Black Bodies, White Bodies: Toward an Iconography of Female Sexuality in Late Nineteenth-Century Art, Medicine, and Literature". In Gates, Henry (Ed.) *Race, Writing and Difference* 223-261. Chicago, University of Chicago Press.

- Gould, Stephen Jay (1985). "The Hottentot Venus". In *The Flamingo's Smile*, 291-305. New York, W.W. Norton and Company. ISBN 0-393-30375-6.

- Strother, Z.S. (1999). "Display of the Body Hottentot", in Lindfors, B., (ed.), *Africans on Stage: Studies in Ethnological Show Business*. Bloomington, Indiana, Indiana University Press: 1-55.

- Qureshi, Sadiah (2004), 'Displaying Sara Baartman, the 'Hottentot Venus', *History of Science* 42:233-257. [1].

7200736R0

Made in the USA
Charleston, SC
03 February 2011